Zapato Power
FREDDIE RAMOS
STOMPS THE SNOW

Jacqueline Jules   art by MIGUEL BENÍTEZ

albert Whitman & Company
Chicago, Illinois

Don't miss the first four **ZaPaTO POWeR** books!

Freddie Ramos Takes Off
Freddie Ramos Springs into action
Freddie Ramos Zooms to the Rescue
Freddie Ramos Makes a Splash

by Jacqueline Jules

illustrated by Miguel Benítez

Library of Congress Cataloging-in-Publication data is on file with the publisher.

Text copyright © 2014 by Jacqueline Jules
Illustrations copyright © 2014 by Miguel Benítez
Published in 2014 by Albert Whitman & Company
ISBN 978-0-8075-9487-2

Printed in China.
10 9 8 7 6 5 4 3 2 1 BP 18 17 16 15 14 13

The design is by Nick Tiemersma.

For more information about Albert Whitman & Company,
visit our web site at www.albertwhitman.com.

To my friends in the
Children's Book Guild
of Washington, D.C.—JJ

zapato power

FREDDIE RAMOS
STOMPS THE SNOW

CONTENTS

1. Too Slippery for Zapato Power? 1

2. A March Blizzard 12

3. The Human Snow Shovel 24

4. The People in Building D 38

5. A Masked Thief 49

6. Cheese in a Mousetrap 57

7. The Giant Pink Purse 67

8. A Lucky Green Cake 75

1. Too Slippery for Zapato Power?

Sparkly white flakes swirled down from the clouds.

"It's sticking!" Geraldo hollered.

Even though it was March, this was the first time we'd seen snow all year. Geraldo, Maria, Jason, and all the kids at recess were jumping for joy. I was too.

"HOORAY!" Jason screamed.

Usually I saved my super-powered sneakers for hero stuff. But I was too excited about the snow. I pressed the button on my Zapato Power wristband. Smoke whooshed out of my shoes, covering me in a cloud.

"Where'd Freddie go?" Maria asked.

Maria couldn't see me bouncing higher than the basketball hoop and sailing over the swing set. **BOING!**

"Freddie!" Maria called for me. "Mrs. Blake says recess is over."

BOING! I landed at Maria's feet and turned off my Zapato Power. It

was time to turn back into a regular kid, even if it was snowing.

"Let's go!" I said to Maria.

When we got into the classroom, Mrs. Blake asked us to open our math books and study for our Friday test. But everyone's eyes, even Mrs. Blake's, kept drifting to the window, where fat snowflakes were falling. First the grass turned white, then the road.

"How much snow do we need to cancel school?" Jason asked.

"In Wisconsin, where I grew up," Mrs. Blake said, "we needed two feet of snow. But around here, it just needs to be slippery outside."

Slippery? Was that good for my super speed? I chewed my pencil.

SCREECH! Something was squealing outside. We dashed out of our seats to watch by the window.

"That blue car is stuck," Mrs. Blake said. "It can't get up the hill."

The snow was making everyone— even our teacher—forget it was math time. Part of me was excited. Slippery roads meant no school and no test tomorrow. The other part of me was worried. If cars couldn't move in the snow, could my super-powered sneakers?

"ANNOUNCEMENT!" The principal's voice came through the

intercom. "SCHOOL WILL BE CLOSING EARLY."

"YAY!" everybody shouted, even Mrs. Blake. I was the only one in the room who wasn't smiling.

Maria and I walked home together. By that time, snow had completely covered the steps leading up to Starwood Park, where we lived.

"Help!" Maria giggled, grabbing the rail.

We couldn't keep from slipping,
and my purple zapatos were soaked.
How could I run at super speed
with wet shoes?

"I need my boots," Maria said.

"At least you have some," I
grumbled.

Maria looked at me. "You don't?"
I shook my head. My super zapatos
were the only shoes I had.

She patted my arm. "Don't worry.

Alonzo probably has some boots that are too small for him."

Maria's big brother, Alonzo, went to high school, and her youngest brother, Gio, was in first grade. Since we were neighbors, Maria's mom let me wear Alonzo's clothes until Gio was big enough for them. At Starwood Park, people shared.

"Keep your fingers crossed for a snow day tomorrow!" Maria said at the door of her apartment, 28G.

I watched her go inside. But I didn't open my door to 29G, even though my nose was a Popsicle and

I knew my guinea pig, Claude the Second, was waiting for me.

The metro train was rumbling by Starwood Park on its overhead track. Claude the Second would understand. There was something important I needed to find out.

I pulled my silver goggles out of my coat pocket and took a big breath. What would happen when I pressed the button on my purple wristband?

ZOOM! ZOOM! ZAPATO!

A puff of smoke cut right through the snowflakes. In half a blink, I was behind Starwood Park, running beside the overhead train track. The train zoomed by! *Rápido!* But not as fast as my Zapato Power!

As I ran, my speed made so much heat that it pushed the curtain of snow away from me and dried up the ground. I went faster and faster,

not feeling cold at all—not even
my nose!

ZOOM! ZOOM! Zapato!

The train fell behind me, just like
every other day with Zapato Power
in my shoes. If someone needed a
superhero, Freddie Ramos would
be ready. But in the meantime, my
guinea pig was waiting for me back
at 29G.

ZOOM! ZOOM! Zapato!

2. A March Blizzard

When I opened the door, my
guinea pig wasn't the only one
waiting.

"Freddie!" Mom frowned. "How
come you didn't come straight
home after school?"

"Mom! How come you're not at
your office?"

"WHEET!" Claude the Second stood up in his cage and squealed. He didn't care who was home first. He wanted his afternoon carrot.

"Everybody canceled because of the storm. We closed the office early."

"So you get a snow day too!" I said.

Mom stopped frowning. "Sí, mi hijito." She kissed my forehead. "Let's have some hot cocoa."

"Great idea!"

While Mom heated the milk, I took off my purple zapatos. They were as dry as a warm blanket. So were my socks. My friend Mr. Vaslov would be happy to hear this. Just because he invented my super shoes didn't mean he knew everything about them. Inventions can do unexpected things. That's why you have to test them. Lucky for me, Mr. Vaslov chose me to be the Zapato Power tester.

We drank our hot cocoa on the couch in front of the television news. A weatherman was standing beside a snow-covered highway with a microphone.

"It's a March blizzard," he said. "Wind gusts of fifty miles per hour are expected as the storm drops almost a foot of snow."

"A whole foot!" Mom put her hands on her cheeks. "And high winds! This sounds serious!"

I turned away from Mom to wink at Claude the Second, munching on his carrot. With Zapato Power, I could take care of us. But Mom didn't know my superhero secret. Shoes with super speed and super bounce are the sort of thing moms think are dangerous. And a good superhero doesn't upset his mom.

"Remember the jigsaw puzzle Uncle Jorge sent me for Christmas?" Mom said.

"The one called Snow Queen?" I asked. "With a thousand pieces?"

"Yes," Mom answered. "This might be a good time to put it together."

We settled down at the table with the puzzle. My job was to find all the straight edge pieces for the border. Mom sorted the different colors. That kept us busy until nine o'clock. In between, we ate dinner and watched the snow through the window. We could see it piling up

on the ground under the sidewalk
lamps. Sometimes it poured out
of the sky in a steady stream.
Other times, the wind roared like
a speeding motorcycle, and snow
blew around in crazy circles.

Just before I went to bed, we watched the news again. The reporter was still outside with his microphone, telling people to stay home. Some people do not listen to their own advice.

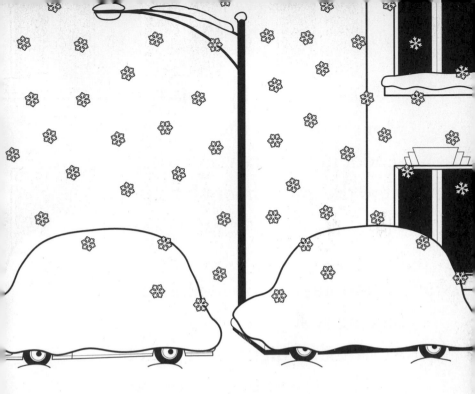

The next morning, I looked
out the window and saw cars
completely buried in snow. The
street had disappeared beneath a
white blanket. So had the sidewalks
and the bushes.

"*Qué bonito.*" I whistled. "Wow!" Mom turned on the news. Every school in the city was closed. So were the government offices and most businesses. It was a snow day for everybody!

"Hooray!" Mom bounced in her blue fuzzy slippers. She was still wearing her nightgown, and her long black hair wasn't combed.

"What do you want to do?" I asked.

Mom yawned. "*Dormir.* Sleep."

"Go back to bed, Mom!" I laughed. "Pretend it's Saturday morning."

While Mom took off her blue slippers and got under the covers, I put on my purple zapatos. There was a big white world outside I wanted to explore.

But first I had to open my front door. I pushed and pushed with my shoulder. Something was blocking me. It was snow!

"The wind made drifts of two feet in some places," a voice behind me said. "People can't get out of their houses."

I looked back at the television. The news reporter was talking about how this was the first time in five years we had a big snow in March.

"Get out and enjoy it, kids!" he said.

I opened the window for another way out. That's when I saw a man in a red hat. It was Mr. Vaslov, my friend who takes care of Starwood Park. He waved a red mitten as he pulled a sled behind him.

"Climb out, Freddie," he said.

Our apartment is on the first floor. With the snow so high, stepping out of the window was almost as easy as stepping out of a bathtub. Mr. Vaslov helped me onto his sled.

"Where are we going?" I asked.

"To my tool shed," Mr. Vaslov said. "I have a new invention to show you."

3. The Human Snow Shovel

Inside the tool shed, Mr. Vaslov moved some tools off his workbench and asked me to sit down.

"Here you go," he said, snapping what looked like mini-sleds under my sneakers. "Zapato Snowshoes."

"Cool!" I said. "What do they do?"

"Let's go outside and see." Mr. Vaslov smiled.

Walking with the snowshoes wasn't easy. I felt like a duck. "The snow is deep, Freddie," Mr. Vaslov pointed around Starwood Park. "People can't get around."

"How can I help?"

"Put on your goggles," he said, "and press the button on your wristband. Starwood Park needs some Zapato Power."

ZOOM! ZOOM! ZaPaTO!

My feet smoked as I zoomed ninety miles an hour in the heavy snow. Everywhere I ran, snow blew out behind me, just like a snow blower.

ZOOM! ZOOM! ZaPaTO!

In less than fifteen minutes, Starwood Park had paths on all the sidewalks, just wide enough for people to get through.

"Your new invention is great!" I told Mr. Vaslov.

"Thanks, Freddie!" He grinned. "Now you can help me rescue some friends."

He put my snowshoes in the tool shed and handed me a shovel. We spent the next hour shoveling out apartments blocked by the snow. When we cleaned Maria's door at 28G, her mother rushed out to kiss us.

"*Gracias, gracias,*" she said.

"*No hay problema.*" I grinned. Sometimes I didn't need Zapato Power to feel like a hero.

Maria came out of 28G wearing pink boots and gloves. Her little brother, Gio, was behind her, pulling a yellow plastic sled.

"Can you go to the hill with us?" he asked.

Mr. Vaslov took my shovel. "I can't. But Freddie can if he asks his mother first."

"Yippee!" Gio yelled, running through the snow paths I'd made on the sidewalks.

By the time we got there, every kid from Starwood Park was at the hill. But most of them were watching because only six kids had sleds.

Gio walked to the top with his yellow sled, then stopped, dead still, his eyes glued on the long way down.

"Have I ever done this before?" he asked.

"Not sure," Maria said. "You might have been too little the last time we had a big snow."

Gio didn't remember sledding. But I remembered the winter my dad came home from being a soldier for a little while. We rode together in the sled, laughing all the way down the hill. I'm proud that my dad was a hero, but I'll always miss him too.

"Do you want me to go with you?" I asked Gio.

"Yes!" He hugged me. Little kids
don't mind being mushy.

We climbed onto the sled and
Maria gave it a push.

"WHEEE!" Gio yelled.

As we swooshed down the hill,
I noticed all the kids without sleds,
watching with big eyes. Suddenly

I had an idea so good, it felt like it came from my super zapatos, not my brain.

"Let's all double up!"

"Then everybody gets a turn!" Maria said.

She asked her friend Jasmin to share. Soon all the kids were pairing up. Now more kids were sledding than watching, with lots of happy cheering.

"Faster! Faster!" Gio shouted all the way down the hill.

At the bottom, he jumped out and grabbed the rope pull. "Let's go again, Freddie!"

"Not so fast!" A girl in a green coat stepped in front of us. "I want a turn!"

The girl chomped on a wad of purple bubblegum. I recognized the grape smell right away. Erika! She was not one of our favorite people at Starwood Park.

"On my sled?" Gio gulped.

"Yeah!" Erika grabbed the rope out of Gio's hand and ran up the hill.

"Stop her!" Gio cried.

It was too late. We waited forever until Erika came back down.

"Here!" She dropped the sled at Gio's feet as she popped a purple bubble. "Your sled is too slow. I'm going to find a better one."

"She didn't even share her ride," Gio griped, picking up the rope.

Keeping as far away from Erika as we could, we went down the hill about a dozen more times. Then Gio walked over to a snowdrift and started digging with his mittens.

"What are you doing?" I asked.

"Building a snow cave," he said. I started to help. Maria came over too. Pretty soon we had a space just big enough for three kids to sit crowded together.

"Who's inside there?" A face

appeared at the cave entrance. We saw a purple mouth and smelled grape bubblegum. Erika!

"Go away!" Gio yelled. "This is our snow cave!"

"Says who!" Erika banged on the top with her fists. Snow fell down on our heads.

"It's crashing in!" we all screamed and crawled out.

By that time, Erika had walked away laughing.

"I'm tired of the way she's always ruining everything," Maria complained.

"Me too!" Gio folded his arms.

I nodded, wondering what I should do about it. Zapato Power was good for running fast. But I needed more than super speed to keep Erika from bothering my friends.

4. The People in Building D

On Saturday morning, Mr. Vaslov rang the doorbell while Mom and I were eating breakfast.

"Sorry to disturb you so early," he said.

"Is something wrong?" Mom asked.

"The furnace in Building D broke."

"In this cold weather?" Mom said. "That's awful!"

Building D was where Erika lived. Did that mean she was shivering? I wondered if I should be sad about that.

"Fire trucks took everyone to Starwood Elementary," Mr. Vaslov said. "They spent the night in the gym. It was on the news."

Camping out at the school? Getting on TV? Why do mean people like Erika have all the luck?

"They need food," Mr. Vaslov said.

"I'll call the neighbors," Mom said. "We'll make meals."

"Thank you," said Mr. Vaslov. "And would you mind if I borrowed

Freddie? There's something he could help me with."

"Of course," said Mom, picking up the phone. "You can have him all day."

Outside, Mr. Vaslov handed
me the zapato snowshoes. "With
people sleeping at the school, we
need a path on the stairs to bring
supplies. How about it, Freddie?"

Mr. Vaslov didn't have to ask me twice. Snow flew everywhere as I zoomed up and down, faster than any machine.

ZOOM! ZOOM! ZAPATO!

In five minutes, the steps between Starwood Park and Starwood Elementary were clean. Mr. Vaslov sprinkled salt on them to keep them from getting icy.

"The sidewalks around the school need clearing too. Are you too tired?"

"*No hay problema*," I said.

ZOOM! ZOOM! ZAPATO!

"Good work, Freddie!"

We walked into the building with a click, clack, clatter.

"Your snowshoes sure are noisy on floors." Mr. Vaslov laughed. He showed me how to fold up the snowshoes and put them in the inside pocket of my winter coat.

"Keep them handy," he said. "You never know when you might need them."

Then we went into the school gym. People immediately surrounded Mr. Vaslov to ask him when the furnace would be fixed in Building D.

"Not before Monday, I'm afraid. We need a new part."

A gray-haired lady with a red wart on her chin turned away with a groan. Then she hobbled off, rubbing her back as if sleeping on the floor hadn't been the best adventure of her life.

"Abuela?" a girl asked. "Are you all right?"

The voice sounded familiar to me but it was a lot nicer than I'd ever heard it before. Bubblegum popped near my ear. I turned to face Erika.

"What are you doing here?" she asked.

"I'm here with Mr. Vaslov," I said, pointing to where people were lined up to talk to him. He was taking notes on a clipboard.

"Last night he came over on the fire trucks with us." She yawned, showing off her purple mouth. "He helped set up the blankets and sleeping bags."

For once, I didn't have to wonder if Erika was telling the truth. Mr. Vaslov always helped the people of Starwood Park.

"Freddie!" He waved at me. "I've got another job for you."

ZOOM! ZOOM! ZAPATO!

For the rest of the afternoon, I ran back and forth between Building D and the school, carrying things Mr. Vaslov pulled out of the apartments for the people camping out in the gym. "We want to make the people of Building D as comfortable as possible," Mr. Vaslov said, checking his clipboard list.

ZOOM! ZOOM! ZAPATO!

That meant finding Pedro's teddy bear in 19D and Mrs. Wu's pillow in 35D. It also meant filling Erika's green backpack with her comb, toothbrush, and purple bubblegum. Eeew! Sometimes being a hero was tough.

ZOOM! ZOOM! ZaPaTO!

I ran back to the school carrying Erika's backpack as far away from my body as possible. My plan was to toss it at her feet, like somebody feeding a lion, and get away in a Zapato

Power flash. But when I walked into the gym, there was crying and commotion.

"MY MONEY!" the gray-haired lady with the red wart on her chin wailed.

"Somebody stole my abuela's purse!" Erika shouted. "Call the police!"

5. A Masked Thief

Mr. Vaslov put away his cell phone. "The police will come as soon as they can. But with the snow, there are emergencies all over the city."

Erika's grandmother covered her face with her wrinkled hands and leaned over like someone about to throw up. I felt sorry for her, even if

she was related to Erika and had a red
wart on her chin.

It got me thinking. Could I do
something? Superheroes helped the
police. But would that be helping
Erika too? Do superheroes have to
help people they don't like?

"Somebody here is a thief!" Erika pointed at the crowd gathering around her grandmother's chair. "Give my abuela's purse back. It has our rent money."

I knew what it was like to worry about rent money. Mom and I did before she got her job at the doctors' office.

"Don't say things like that," Mr. Vaslov told Erika. "We're all neighbors here."

Was there anyone in the school right now who didn't live at Starwood Park? It was time to do a little Zapato Power snooping.

ZOOM! ZOOM! ZAPATO!

Right away, I spotted footprints—
lots of them—up and down the hall
by the back gym door. Were they
all from the people in Building D?
Or did one set of footprints belong
to a crook?

ZOOM! ZOOM! ZAPATO!

I searched the rest of the school.
Most of the halls were dark. I saw
only one light coming from a boys'
bathroom. Then it clicked off. I took

two steps closer. That's when I felt cold air in the hallway. Was there a thief near me...or...a ghost? Superheroes are supposed to be brave. But they don't have to do everything alone. I ran back to the gym for help.

ZOOM! ZOOM! ZAPATO!

"Mr. Vaslov!" I tugged on his arm. "Can I show you something?"

He followed me right away. Mr. Vaslov wasn't like some grown-ups who didn't listen to kids. "I'm glad you came for me, Freddie."

And I was glad I had Mr. Vaslov by my side as we tiptoed down the darkest hall of the school. Mr. Vaslov switched on the light in the boys' bathroom.

"The window is open," Mr. Vaslov said. "Looks like somebody made a getaway."

We looked around for other clues.

"Look!" I pointed. "A blue ski mask!"

Mr. Vaslov picked it up. "This could be important!"

"Does anyone at Starwood Park wear a ski mask?" I asked.

"Not that I know of," Mr. Vaslov said. "Let's go ask around."

In the hallway, we heard shouting again.

"My purse! Who took my purse?" It was my mom's voice. I'd forgotten she was coming to Starwood Elementary to bring food to the people of Building D. Did the thief get her purse too?

6. Cheese in a Mousetrap

The police came to investigate the purse stolen from Erika's grandmother and found out about Mom's missing purse too. They got a two-for-one deal.

"My bag was there," Mom told Officer Sanchez. She pointed to the wall near the door. "I put it down to fix the food on the table."

Mom stood beside plates of enchiladas, refried beans, yucca, and guacamole. Neighbors at Starwood Park had made all those dishes for the people of Building D.

"Was there money in your purse?" Officer Chen asked.

"Yes," Mom answered sadly. "One hundred dollars. Money collected to buy more food for the people of Building D."

"The thief stole charity?" Officer Sanchez asked.

Mom nodded. "It's in a brown envelope."

"And what color was your purse?" Officer Chen asked.

"Yellow." Mom pulled on her long black ponytail, something she always did when she was upset.

Officer Sanchez turned to the crowd gathered around them. "Did anyone else see anything?"

"Freddie did." Mr. Vaslov stepped up and showed the officers the blue ski mask.

"Where did you find this?" Officer Chen looked excited.

Mr. Vaslov and I rushed down the hall with the officers to the boys' bathroom. We all looked out the open window. There was a set of snow prints leading to a shoveled sidewalk.

"Look at those three houses over there." Mr. Vaslov pointed. "Do you think the thief lives in one of them?"

"Maybe," said Officer Sanchez. "We've been tracking a school purse snatcher for months now. He's hit six other schools already."

"We call him the Serial School Purse Snatcher," Officer Chen said.

"Keep your eyes open. Let us know if you see something suspicious. We'd really like to catch this thief." Officer Sanchez waved as he and Officer Chen left the school.

The police needed someone to snoop! I grinned. My super zapatos made me the perfect guy for the job.

ZOOM! ZOOM! ZAPATO!

In half a blink, I was outside, looking at the three houses we saw from the bathroom window. The first one had a white porch. The second one had green shutters. And the third one was redbrick. All three houses were quiet with no lights on.

This was like the footprints. How can you tell a crook's house

from an honest person's house? If I
jumped, could I see more through
the windows? I pressed the second

button on my wristband, the one that gave me super bounce.

BOING!
BOING!
BOING!

I bounced up and down the sidewalk, my Zapato Power smoke swirling around me. The smoke didn't just make me invisible; it gave me special vision, like looking through a telescope. If a crook was counting stolen money in one of those houses, my Zapato Power eyes would spot it.

BOING!
BOING!
BOING!

In the house with the porch, I saw two bedrooms. Both of them had blankets and sheets thrown every which way. The house with green shutters had dirty dishes all over the kitchen table. The brick house had clothes on the floor of the living room. Some people don't have moms who make them clean up.

BOING!
BOING!
BOING!

Just because my mom liked things clean didn't mean the police would arrest someone for being messy. They needed something more suspicious, and I wasn't finding it just jumping around. This job needed more than Zapato Power—it needed brainpower too. I sat on the school steps to think.

What did the Serial School Purse Snatcher want? That was an easy one. He wanted purses! What if I left one out on the sidewalk? Wouldn't that be like putting cheese in a mousetrap?

It was a good idea with one big

problem. I pressed the button on my purple wristband to solve it.

ZOOM! ZOOM! ZAPATO!

Two blinks later, I was knocking at 28G. Maria answered the door.

"Can I borrow a purse?" I asked.

7. The Giant Pink Purse

Maria had a huge pink purse that used to belong to her mother.

"I'll let you borrow it on one condition," she said.

That condition meant I had to let her be a part of my plan.

"Policemen like a second witness," she said. "Don't you watch TV?"

Maria had a point.

"And purses are usually carried by girls," she added.

I hadn't thought about that.

"Okay," I told Maria. "You can be my partner."

"Great!" she said. "Let's get Gio."

"Why do we need Gio?"

"I promised Mama I'd pick him up at the sledding hill," Maria answered.

A few minutes later, we were listening to Gio cry.

"I don't want to stop sledding!" His face was so red from the cold that he looked like a cherry.

"Aren't you hungry?" I asked. "There's great food in the gym."

"They have guacamole," Maria said.

Gio stopped crying and turned his cherry face up. "Let's go!"

Some people can be bought with guacamole. Gio is one of them.

When we got to the gym, everyone was eating off green plates and wiping their mouths with green napkins. I saw a big green cake in the shape of a four-leaf clover on the table. It had a rainbow with a pot of gold on it.

"That looks like one lucky cake," I said. "Where did it come from?" "A nice man at the supermarket," Mom said. "He saw the news story on the TV and thought we might like to celebrate St. Patrick's Day a little early."

"Why not?" I said, picking up a green plate.

Superheroes are always on the job, but they still need to eat. Maria followed me to the table with the giant pink purse dangling off her arm. Gio was right behind her.

"Guacamole!" Gio smiled. "My favorite!"

As he piled up his plate, Erika came over and cut into line.

"Hey!" she said. "Leave some for other people."

This was the third time in two days Erika had bothered Gio. With Gio, it's three strikes and you're out. He put his arms around the guacamole bowl.

"You can't have any," he shouted. "You're a bully!"

"Gio," Maria warned. "That might not be a good idea."

It all happened faster than Zapato Power. Gio took the guacamole and dashed out the gym door. Erika tried to stop him. Maria went to save him. They all grabbed at the bowl. Before I could blink, guacamole was all over Erika, Gio, and Maria.

"Yuck!" Erika said, wiping green stuff off her face.

"Double yuck!" Maria said, dropping her pink purse in the hall-way. It was covered in guacamole too.

We all ran to grab green napkins.
By the time we came back, the
guacamole-covered purse was gone!
   "Call the police!" Maria cried,
wiping mushy stuff off her shirt.
Some grown-ups took out their cell
phones as Mr. Vaslov rushed over
to us.

"What happened?" he asked, staring at Erika's face. She had guacamole on her eyebrows.

"Get me more napkins!" she demanded.

Gio ran away to hug his mother. I pressed the button on my wristband. It was time to get out of there.

ZOOM! ZOOM! ZAPATO!

8. A Lucky Green Cake

The Serial School Purse Snatcher had a head start. No hay problema. There was a trail of green guacamole in the snow.

ZOOM! ZOOM! ZaPaTo!

I followed the tiny blobs of green around the corner. But that's where the trail ended.

"Did you see where he went?" Mr. Vaslov asked, catching up with me.

I shook my head. "He just disappeared."

"Put on your snowshoes, Freddie," Mr. Vaslov said. "They might help us."

With my Zapato Power snowshoes, I was ready to chase the purse snatcher through the snow. But I had to find him first.

"Look closely for guacamole." Mr. Vaslov peered down at the white ground.

We walked down the block toward
the bus stop. That's where we saw
another spot of green.

"Do you think the thief got away on the bus?" I asked.

"I don't know. Let's keep looking."

Behind the bus stop was a park. We saw some footprints going around the trunk of a big tree.

"What's that?" I pointed at a mound of snow.

"We'll find out!" Mr. Vaslov said.

When we got there, we saw someone had made a snow cave, just like Gio had on the sledding hill. But instead of kids playing inside, there were stolen purses. We saw a yellow purse, a pink one,

and a third
one that
I figured
belonged
to Erika's
grandmother.
"The thief's
hideout!" Mr. Vaslov whistled.
But where was the thief? I turned
around to see a tall, thin man in
a blue coat running toward the
bus stop. And the bus was coming
down the street!

ZOOM! ZOOM! ZAPATO!

I ran around him in circles,
smoke flying everywhere. Just like a
snowplow, I pushed enough snow to
lock him into a snow jail.

"Hey! Where did this come from!?" the man shouted.

Mr. Vaslov ran up. "That's our thief all right. He has guacamole on his jacket."

We heard sirens and saw a police car pull up in front of the school. "Go tell the officers where we are," Mr. Vaslov said. "Tell them to bring shovels."

"Sure thing!" I said, pressing the button on my wristband.

ZOOM! ZOOM! ZAPATO!

Maria, Gio, Erika, her grandmother, my mom, and just about

everyone else from Building D came to watch Officers Chen and Sanchez arrest the Serial School Purse Snatcher.

"How long did you think you could get away with this?" Officer Chen asked as he handcuffed the thief.

The Serial School Purse Snatcher hung his head so no one could see his face.

"Starwood Park is safe again," Mom said.

Mr. Vaslov quietly patted me on the back.

After that, we all went back to the gym to have lucky green cake.

"Yum," Gio said, licking his fingers. "This is as good as guacamole. Green must be a good color for food."

The next morning, Maria, Gio, and I went to the sledding hill with all the other kids from Starwood Park. The sun was so bright, we hardly got cold.

Mr. Vaslov came too with some clean trash can lids so we had more sleds to share. That put everyone in an extra good mood, even Erika. She didn't say a mean thing all day. In fact, at the top of the hill, she told Gio and me to go down the hill first.

"How come?" I asked, just to be sure she wasn't planning to crash into us or anything.

"I owe you one," she said, popping a purple bubble.

So we zoomed down the hill in front of Erika, cheering all the way.

WHeee!

ZAPATO POWER
THE ADVENTURES
OF FREDDIE RAMOS

"Engaging and fast-paced, this title will bait
many young imaginations, particularly among
the Flat Stanley crowd."—*School Library Journal*

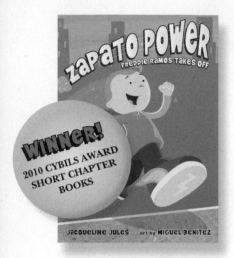

One day Freddie Ramos comes home from school and finds a strange box just for him. What's inside?

HC 9780807594803
$14.99/$16.99 Canada
PB 9780807594797
$4.99/$5.99 Canada

In this sequel, Freddie has shoes that give him super speed. It's hard to be a superhero and a regular kid at the same time, especially when your shoes give you even more power!

HC 9780807594810
$14.99/$16.99 Canada
PB 9780807594834
$4.99/$5.99 Canada

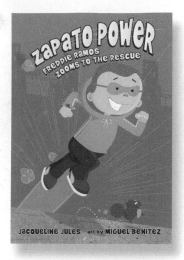

Freddie's super-speedy adventures continue—now he has superhero duties at school!

HC 9780807594827
$14.99/$16.99 Canada
PB 9780807594841
$4.99/$5.99 Canada

When Freddie's zapatos go missing, how can he use his zapato power?

HC 9780807594858
$14.99/$16.99 Canada
PB 9780807594865
$4.99/$5.99 Canada

Jacqueline Jules is the author of more than twenty books, including *Zapato Power: Freddie Ramos Takes Off*, which won a Cybils Award. She is also a poet, teacher, and librarian. Visit her at www.jacquelinejules.com.

Miguel Benítez likes to describe himself as a part-time daydreamer and a full-time doodler. He lives with his wife and two cats in England.